```
FIC     Ferguson, William,
        1943-

        Freedom and other
        fictions
```

DATE		

CHICAGO PUBLIC LIBRARY
HILD REGIONAL
4455 LINCOLN AVE.
CHICAGO, ILLINOIS 60625

© THE BAKER & TAYLOR CO.

Freedom and Other Fictions

William Ferguson

FREEDOM

AND OTHER
FICTIONS

Alfred A. Knopf   New York   1984

This Is a Borzoi Book
Published by Alfred A. Knopf, Inc.

Copyright © 1980, 1981, 1982, 1983, 1984 by
William Ferguson
All rights reserved under International and
Pan-American Copyright Conventions.
Published in the United States by
Alfred A. Knopf, Inc., New York, and
simultaneously in Canada by Random House
of Canada Limited, Toronto. Distributed by
Random House, Inc., New York.

Certain of the stories in this collection have
appeared previously in the following publications:
Canton, *Fiction*, and *Malahat Review*. "A Summer
at Estabrook," "Morrissey," and "Dies Irae"
first appeared in *The Paris Review*.

Library of Congress Cataloging in Publication Data
Ferguson, William, [date]
Freedom and other fictions.
I. Title.
PS3556.E72F7   1984   813'.54   83-48852
ISBN 0-394-53391-7

Manufactured in the United States of America
First Edition

for Nancy

Contents

Morrissey   3

Cortez   11

Dies Irae   15

Terror   19

The Third Voice   25

A Summer at Estabrook   29

The Family   43

Space Invaders   45

Contents

Scherzo with TV Antenna   49

The Claims Adjuster   57

Freedom   67

The Teacher   73

Freedom and Other Fictions

Morrissey

There was a pianist living across the street from us this past summer who used to play the same Schubert sonata that's on your record, the posthumous B-flat major. I think he may have had the same recording, or one very much like it; sometimes you'd hear him stop practicing and then after a minute the same music would start up again, but this time with a quality of, how shall I say, of great goodness, which makes me think it may have been the Rubinstein you have there in your hand. Don't ask me what I mean by great goodness, because I don't know, and even repeating the words this one time they begin to sound sentimental, and that's not the point. It was just a quality that was lacking in Morrissey's playing, and since his technique was excellent, and his heart seemed to be in it, so that short passages could take your breath away, it's very difficult to say what this lack consisted of entirely. (That's an odd turn of phrase, isn't it? —the idea that a lack could consist of something.) I think it may have been his handling of tempo. He had the bad habit of rushing certain passages, in a way typical of students who've reached an advanced level of competence without ever realizing that eventually they must be not only very competent but very good. And there we are again at that word. People say "good musician" when what they mean is "competent." Morrissey was extremely competent; Rubinstein is extremely good. The difference is everything; it's the difference between real music and —well, what we ordinarily have to put up with.

Morrissey had a musicologist friend at Harvard— Robert Weston, I think his name was—who once used a computer to measure the accuracy of several great pianists. Rubinstein finished last, of course, in close competition with Serkin; at the top of the list was the icy Glenn Gould. (In defense of Professor Weston, it should be observed that although he did publish the results of his experiment, the conclusion he drew was one that any concertgoer would quickly agree with, namely that the degree of technical accuracy in pianists of a certain rank is not particularly significant.) When Morrissey told me all this, I said I was surprised that his friend hadn't gone a little further and hypothesized that really good music-making is always marked by obvious technical flaws, and that perhaps they were there by some sort of design, in the same way the Indians of Panama are careful to avoid perfect symmetries in the patterns of their textiles (I used some such fatuous comparison); after all, the two pianists who supposedly had the most trouble with technique were precisely the most graceful ones, the ones who took your breath away in concert. It seems that Morrissey had made some such observation to Weston, but in more intelligent terms than mine (I admit now that no sane pianist would ever deliberately sabotage his own execution); and he asked what exactly had been measured by the computer in regard to tempo? Percentage of notes played at precisely the right moment, composer-indicated ritardandi, fermate, and so on excepted, said Weston, not without misery. Morrissey: then if the pianist respects the indicated tempo overall in a given passage, but the individual notes have, as it were, an organic rather than a mechanical relationship to the larger scheme, his marks will still be low? Not really, said Weston, or just low according to my wretched system; anyway, what do you understand by *organic* and *mechanical*? Maybe those aren't the best words for it, said Morrissey, but surely you'll agree that a given handling of tempo might satisfy my organic ear—influenced, as it is, by fluctuating natural rhythms—at the same time your computer's mechanical ear is rejecting it. The public is human, after all, not a machine. The columns of the Parthenon swell at the center to satisfy the human eye; they were not shaped to please a republic of measuring sticks. (My comparison had not been the only fatuous one, it seems; it was obvious that Morrissey had not yet read Kamienski on the rubato.) I've forgotten how the professor is supposed to have responded to this. But the discussion was superfluous, in any case; Weston's private view was that his own research was worthless, except perhaps as a warning to younger scholars.

The sound of a piano is very penetrating—unavoidable, you might say—but at the same time it seems to us to be one of the most tolerable of instruments, at the other end of the spectrum from, say, the violin-playing of our upstairs tenant, whom we're trying to evict, by the way. So we didn't mind Morrissey particularly, even when we were trying to work and he was playing, even when, as I say, he would vary the tempo so rashly in the first movement of the Schubert. When I think about it more carefully, I realize that it did bother me in principle, but that I forgave him very early and forever for all such transgressions, so that they became, as it were, inaudible. I remember the first day I heard him play; it was a very warm evening, surprisingly so for the beginning of June, and our block was taking on some of the qualities of a real neighborhood—children crying on balconies, dogs being walked, hibachi smoke drifting pleasantly among the old frame houses. I began to hear the Schubert; it seemed to be coming through an open window across the street. The first melody was well played, strong and brave, but then, as it appeared to fail—I mean after the first statement, when a development should begin but does not really begin—the unseen pianist started to rush, as if he had lost his bearings and was being carried helplessly forward by a river without a name; there were excitements, as always, but of the adolescent kind—the quick green spasms of the very young, so to speak, which are only tolerable against the promise of a long, and unproven, life of real sensuality. Now he slowed, as if realizing his mistake, but it was as if he could no longer imagine the original tempo. I crossed the street on the pretext of mailing a letter; now I heard a metronome ticking, like Japanese bones in the wind; now nothing at all; and now the sweeter, surer notes of a musician of great goodness. I found myself imagining an eighteen-year-old, a twenty-year-old at most, behind the shade in desperate frustration, on the bench, listening once again to the inimitable notes of the master. As I passed the house, the shade was suddenly lifted, the window opened wider, and I saw the pianist leaning out, as if inside he hadn't been able to breathe.

I stared at him in surprise: the man was over forty. His face was curiously soft, even in the tension of the moment; he opened his mouth unnecessarily wide, as if the need for great drafts of air had been accompanied by a compulsion to somehow dramatize his anger, at least to himself; or it may have been a genuine anxiety attack of the type I was to see him suffer later in the summer, when we had become friends. In those frightful episodes, his heart would suddenly begin to race and drive him out of his chair; the automatic dilation of his lungs seemed to have stopped, so that he had to struggle for every breath; blushing scarlet, gasping, panicky, he lurched and reeled from corner to corner and throughout the house, appealing to us for help that we could not possibly give, because we knew that physically there was nothing wrong. The attack would pass after an hour or so, which usually included a walk around the block, Morrissey tottering terrified between us, wanting to run away, as we held tight on either side and kept up a steady rhythm of talk to see if we could somehow bring him back to normal.

And before long he would be fine. After a day or two, there would be shamefaced apologies and effusive thanks. But how exhausting it was!—physically, I mean. The curious thing is that we never had any strong emotional reaction to Morrissey's bad times, as you would have expected, given their violent character. We couldn't help wondering about the rest of his life, and the bearing it might have on the problem, and so we asked him in detail about his family and friends, his childhood in Minnesota, his ex-wife, about the silent side of the musician, so to speak. Most of the time, even when he was perfectly calm, Morrissey was not very open on these subjects, except insofar as they had to do with a favorite maxim—namely, that the most important thing in life is not to repeat yourself. He did not put it quite so simply; he would say "not to repeat your mistakes," but it was clear to us that he had very little idea what he meant by a mistake; his relationship with his father had certainly been disastrous, but to say that one or the other of the parties had been in error would have been impossible, to judge from what he told us; yet the unhappiness of the memory had prevented him from forming any close relationships with the kind of surrogate fathers we all seem to find in uncles, teachers, elder colleagues, and so on. It was the same with his marriage, which had lasted barely a year (when he was nineteen!); he would begin to sound knowledgeable and world-weary as he described his months of married life, but we couldn't for the life of us connect his self-evident truths to any experience of ours, or anything else we'd ever heard of. After a while, we began to understand what his principle of non-repetition really meant—and it was not that he claimed to have understood his mistakes and was determined not to have them happen again; no, by refusing to "repeat," he simply wanted to avoid giving people the impression that he was incapable of growth and change. It was on this monstrous triple negative, this social sham, that his life was built. It goes without saying that his terror of repetition itself constituted a pattern, and a particularly rigid one, a system of avoidances; but Morrissey didn't see it that way; he seemed to think of life as something that, by definition, happened elsewhere, from which his own rhythm of activity was somehow exempt.

I don't mean to be hard on poor Morrissey; I'm only

trying to tell the truth. I think there would have been much more sympathy from us if he had seemed more real, or more believable, but in fact there was always a sheen of irreality about him, even in the thick of a mental crisis; so that even though we were doing our best to cope with a difficult situation, we did not seem to be more than superficially moved by it.

What I've said is not quite right; almost, but not quite. Let me see whether I can explain. I was talking about the first time I heard Morrissey play, when I saw him leaning out the window. The revelation was not that he was middle-aged. It was the face that shocked me. Have you ever seen those strange adolescents—say from age fifteen on—who should be beautiful in promise but who instead give the impression of being permanently unrealized? Adults are always depressed at the sight of them, because every conceivable element of beauty is present except grace, and in the absence of grace, which I suppose is the genius for living and moving in time, it suddenly becomes apparent that nothing else matters. Morrissey's face was like that, but much older; it was perfect, everything admirable seemed to be combined in those features, and so there was no possible way to deny that his face was beautiful, except for the bald statement that it was not. Not that it was ugly; rather unreal, like a frozen child's. When I first saw it, I immediately forgave this stranger for all his inabilities—his failure to keep to any rhythm, organic or otherwise, to bring some kind of reasonable order to those long landscapes of the Viennese, to comprehend and administer time and hold it safely in his hands; I forgave Morrissey for all this and more, I mean to say that I gave him up for dead.

Cortez

It looks exactly like you; no one knows what to make of it. According to one of the scouts who came back this morning, this jointed simulacrum of your body, or whatever it is, moving slowly toward the Spanish encampment through the dunes, may have been sent by Montezuma to nullify the magic of your illegal advance. Like the sheen of evil over a failed harvest, the sun gleams on its forearms, which seem to be made of golden oak but which move like human limbs and even perspire. Pieces of excrement drop from its buttocks as it walks; it is clearly not human, yet still some kind of animal, unless it really is made of oak and all this is merely artifice. It smiles as it approaches you; its face is unquestionably yours, as you have come to know it over the years, but reversed on its axis, with the so-called male half where the female should be, and vice versa. Two priests are in at-

Cortez

tendance, one on each side; it is not clear whether they support the image or whether it walks alone. Now it stands facing you, grinning horribly, and offers you its tightly closed left hand with the knuckles turned upward. You conceal your feelings; you take pains to greet it ceremoniously, perhaps to convince the priests of the clear difference between you, though it seems unnecessary, as the wooden image is naked and brown and you are fully clothed and city-white. Near the end of your remarks the statue suddenly urinates, soaking your woolen leggings, which begin to stink in the sun. Your soldiers edge forward, flushed with anger; you resist the temptation to strike out; instead, you lean forward and examine his face, which is unchanging as if carven; you see it was not meant as an insult; you compose yourself. The two priests nod their heads in relief. Now with the fingertips of his right hand he touches your eyes with unexpected gentleness, like a blind person; his left hand, still shut tight, is pressed against your navel. You are not surprised at his familiarity; it is as if the hand were your own; you even feel your whole body scald and shrivel, the price of solitude in this disastrous century. Now he backs off somewhat, and the sun turns the color of milk; the clenched left hand is again held forward; it looks strangely mild, like a sack of ancient poison in a museum case. The palm opens; among the familiar creases lies your life; it is like a drop of something between water and mercury, which seems to evaporate as it spreads between the fingers; you try to grasp it, already breathless at the intuition of failure, and find yourself holding a dry hand that is indeed made of wood; the priests move quickly forward as if on signal; the Spaniards are motionless as if frozen; your eyes are somehow spared as your body is cut down; you keep staring into the sky as if it were tiled with silver coins.

The adjutant Sandoval wakes you to the realities of Vera Cruz, this legal fiction of yours which the Emperor may or may not recognize. Your presence is required; the Mexicans have sent an imperial delegation; one of its members has nearly caused a riot; he stands half hidden among the other Indians, but the phenomenon is too striking to miss, one would have to be blind; he is your double, sir, he looks like you in every particular down to his fingernails, except of course that you are heavily tanned from the Cuban sun and he is quite pale, perhaps an albino. The men are very anxious; what do you advise?

Outside the canvas the soldiers are arguing among themselves; here and there you hear an incongruous shout of laughter. You open the tent flap, still bleary-eyed, and look out into the blinding American sun; at the sight of you, there is utter silence. Without a word, unarmed, you stride into the midst of the delegation; you see immediately that the albino has no resemblance to you at all; he cowers before you like a rabbit; you know you must act quickly and decisively or you will be lost, as in the dream; in a single motion, you pull his obsidian dagger from its sheath and make a deep diagonal slash in the monster's chest; the Spaniards stiffen in surprise; the other Indians have disappeared, there is only white sky—but no, you look down, the Indians have fallen like silk at your feet; now you are truly a god, not even the Emperor Charles can deny it now. The albino's mouth gapes in a rictus of pain; you enlarge the wound; the blood spurts in your face and blinds you as your hand penetrates to the living heart, rips it from its paltry armature, and holds it fast over your bloody head in triumph; the albino's body

Cortez

slumps away, still twitching marvelously as if alive, and all at once you understand that the adjutant was right, the creature is a perfect double of yourself, down to its fingernails, which claw now in spasms at the desiccated earth below your booted feet.

Sandoval lingers at your tent, a harquebus-shot from where you stand in glory, but his face is as clear as a diamond, it seems to grow in size and float away from his body, now soaring over the camp like an eagle, now hovering over your head in wonder at what you have dared to do, and, as you watch, his shocked expression turns to joy, then to confusion, and finally to fatigue, as if he were saying: it has been no use, the Emperor has forgotten you and me and all we did for Spain. This is not the Indies; you are sitting in the anteroom of the palace, still unable to see His Majesty after all these weeks. Sandoval bends over you, alarmed as he sees you clutching your heart. You reassure him; you attempt to get up, but sink back helplessly onto the hated velvet. Sandoval offers his hand to help you; after a moment's hesitation, you accept it. In the features of his loyal face, exhausted, ineffectual, and old, you seem to see your own.

Dies Irae

Sunday, July 11th.

My wife says it would be nice to win the lottery because then we could pay off the second mortgage. I tell her that the odds she's counting on for that are the same ones that make it unlikely she'll be slammed in the head by a meteor on the way to work. She doesn't seem to be terribly impressed with this line of reasoning. She says she's never really been bothered by the thought of being struck by a body from the heavens. She says that there is every expectation she will be struck by a good meteor and not a bad meteor when a meteor gets around to striking her.

Maybe I didn't explain myself very well.

Dies Irae

Monday, July 12th.

It would have been fantastically improbable for someone to come up to me when I was twenty-one (say) and baldly put the question of what I had done with my life up to then (not that no one ever asked the question when I was that age; they did, repeatedly, but obviously no one ever meant it; they just couldn't have). The question *would have made sense* at twenty-one, I want to make that clear —that's why I always felt a shudder when anyone went through the motions of asking it ("What have you been doing with yourself?" etc.).

Unfortunately, the longer you live, the more likely it gets that someone, sometime, will look you up and down with a truly objective eye and make a judgment. We may feel, with every decade that passes, that the odds of this happening have gone from one in a million to one in a hundred thousand or one in ten thousand. But the fact is that we have no idea how the odds shift, or what they were in the first place.

Maybe that's why I'm so nervous today, and I really am, I have to admit it. Do you know what it's like to intuit that the Day of Judgment is not far off? That it might come today? This very morning? In the slow rain, as you walk to perform errands whose importance you only vaguely grasp, a day when the simplest tasks seem impossible, surely no day to defend the indefensible, and not outside, not in this weather.

Tuesday 13th.

Raquel has just won the lottery.

It's a small amount compared to the grand prize, but large enough to pay off the second mortgage and have quite a bit left over.

The strange thing is that she had no premonition of success, and she's famous for the accuracy of her premonitions.

I've decided to ask Raquel for the extra winnings, to start a new career for myself. I don't know what, not yet. But I just have to get out of this city. I can't stand this weather—every raindrop is like a tiny, sullen mirror. I must see my face reflected a thousand times a day. It looks so pale and prismatic, so unspeakably small.

Terror

I haven't decided whether I want to go back to camp this summer. I know Jim is going. But I don't think he likes me anymore. Something went wrong last year around mid-season. I mean, I did something wrong—and after that, it was never the same. I don't even know why it was so terrible. All I know is, I lost my best friend.

I never had a really close friend like that before.

He was someone I cared about a lot more than I did about myself. The other thing is, I tried to be with him as much of the time as possible, like when we went down to the lake for morning swim.

The rule for buddies was that you just paired off with whoever was next to you. But Jim and I used to arrange it so we always ended up holding hands by the time they opened the gate and let us out on the dock.

Terror

    Our cabin leader would get angry sometimes and tell us to split up and meet some new people.

    But we didn't care. We went together every day, even when it was raining and you practically froze until the leaders blew the whistle and you could get into the water where it felt warm under the raindrops.

    On the good days, Jim and I would swim for a while and then get out and sun ourselves on the boards. When they blew buddy-check, we could lie there and hold up our hands without even opening our eyes.

    We felt special, because we were the only two full-season campers in the whole Intermediate Division. Around the third week in July, everybody else went home, and we were left alone together for a few hours until the new boys came. We knew most of them from other years, anyway. But they still seemed like newcomers. We showed them around like guides and pointed out all the things that had been done since they'd been gone.

    I was proud of the camp. That's why it hurt so much when I let everybody down. I still don't know how I could do a thing like that—but I did, and I guess I have to accept the consequences.

It happened one night at Orientation Lodge, when the director and all the leaders introduce themselves to the second-month campers. Jim and I had to come too, since we already knew everybody and were supposed to lead the cheers. They stood up one by one, the director said a few choice words, and we all had to react as if we were in love with them. I looked over at our leader, Ken Eastwood; he was sitting at the end of the table in his whites, teetering back in his chair a little and gazing out over the lake as he waited his turn. He looked like one of those pictures you see in college catalogues.

That's when I had a bright idea. I leaned over to Jim and whispered in his ear: "What if when Kenny gets up, we boo him instead?"

Jim laughed, bouncing up and down a little in that special way he had. "Go ahead," he said.

"Will you do it with me?"

There was no time for an answer. "Ken Eastwood, Cabin Twelve," said the director. "Let's hear it for Kenny!"

"Boo!" I shouted.

Actually, it was pretty funny. I felt like a hero. Even the leaders were laughing, all except Ken.

Then the director got up again, looking grave. The silence in the room was complete.

"I don't want to ruin anybody's fun," he said, "but before we go any further, I want to explain a camp tradition to the new boys. There is no booing at Beechwood." He paused impressively to let it sink in. "I'm sure Bobby meant it as a joke. But it was in very poor taste, and it would seem he owes Ken a personal apology."

Everyone had moved away from me now, even Jim. I couldn't seem to speak.

"We're waiting," said the director.

"I'm sorry," I said. "It was only a joke."

Without looking me in the eye, Ken managed a thin smile. "Apology accepted," he said. "I'm glad we've cleared up this little misunderstanding, and I don't hold grudges."

I could see he was still angry, but I didn't know what else to do.

The director explained that no one should blame me for what I'd done, since we're all human and anyone can make a mistake; why didn't we just forget it and learn some of the camp songs. He led off with "Boola Boola." I began to sing along to see if I could get over my embarrassment—I was supposed to be helping the new boys learn the music, after all—but the other campers glared at me, and after a while I figured it was better to keep quiet.

No one spoke to me as we walked back up through the grove to the cabins. I saw Jim with some other boys, so far ahead of me it was impossible to catch up. By the time I got there, he had already undressed and gone to bed with his face to the wall. I climbed up to my bunk, right above his, and then stuck my head over the side.

"Jim?" I said.

"What do you want?"

"I hope Kenny knows I was only kidding."

"He knows," said Jim. "Just go to sleep."

Ken came in a few minutes later to make sure he had us all safely in bed. We lay there quietly. When he was satisfied, he told us to sleep well and turned off the light.

But he didn't leave. At first, I couldn't tell where he was in the darkness; then I heard the floorboards creaking under his sneakers next to my bunk. He bent close to my ear.

"I was disappointed in you tonight, Bobby," he said in a stage whisper.

"I know," I said. "I'm sorry."

"Can you think of any reason I should feel differently?"

"It was only supposed to be a joke," I said.

I could hear Jim turn on the lower bunk.

"I'm going to watch you very closely from now on," said Ken. "All the leaders are, after tonight."

There were none of the usual sounds from the rest of the cabin. I knew everybody was listening.

"You seem to have quite a bit of trouble making friends," Ken said. "Why do you suppose that is?"

"I have a lot of friends," I answered.

"I'm talking about real friends, Bobby. Who are your real, true friends?" Ken said.

"I'm friends with Jim," I said.

"No, he's not," I heard Jim say from the darkness below.

"You see?" Ken said.

I didn't dare turn my head. I just lay there staring up. I couldn't feel his breath on my cheek anymore, and I thought maybe he'd gone away.

"What I want you to do," he said after a while, "is to think it over and decide whether you're really cut out to be a camper here. If the answer is yes, and we can see some changes in your attitude, I think everything may turn out all right. And you can count on me to help you."

He didn't sound so angry anymore, and I asked him whether he was still my friend.

He said yes.

I lay there wondering how come Jim was still mad if Ken had forgiven me. That's what I'm still wondering about.

The Third Voice

There are two hills on my farm, both heavily wooded. One is near the house; the other is at the far end of the property, down by the river. When I climb the near hill in the early morning, there seems to be a man shouting from the far one. I shout back, but he never answers. So I hike down toward the river and up the other slope, but no one is ever there, and I hear the shouting again from the first hill. This has been going on, winter and summer, since my son moved his family to Boston, seven years ago this March.

I know the man I hear is the ghost of a suicide: my grandfather, John Rudd, who owned this farm before I was born. He was a good man, but given to alcohol. One day his wife and children left him for better things; a week later, John hanged himself in the barn—the one I still use today.

The Third Voice

In the evenings, I get to thinking about John Rudd; I go into the barn after supper and stare up at the rafters, wondering what it would be like to die.

Before my son left, I remember, we all used to walk up on the hill at dusk and hoot at the great horned owl that lived in the hemlocks. We had no idea what we were saying, of course, but whatever it was, the bird was saying it back.

The exchange with my grandfather is more disturbing. One word from me is enough to quiet him; his silence makes me giddy, like the dizziness that comes over me when I'm plowing the middle field and the woodlot begins to go yellow and brittle at the edges, like a page in an old book.

It bothers me to think that my grandfather and I may be striding through each other's bodies as we cross in the morning, as insubstantial, at least to each other's eyes, as dust off the summer fields.

"Hold your horses," he seems to be saying. "Hold your horses!"

Is he telling me to wait? Why should I wait?

There is a third voice, sometimes, that comes from the field across the river. It is certainly not an echo of John Rudd's; it sounds more like a child calling its father.

The land is beautiful over there, rich and level, with no stones. When my son comes back, he should buy it any way he can and repair the bridge, because it would make all the difference, and maybe then he'd have something worthwhile to give his children.

I've told him so.

But he doesn't answer letters.

I lean on a fencepost, gazing across the river.

"Coming!" says the voice from over there. "I'm coming!"

I hear it, as I hear John Rudd; but I say nothing. What good would it do? These voices, by now, are as familiar and useless as wind in the swaying trees.

A Summer at Estabrook

I realize of course that I'm no longer worthy of the name musician, if ever I was, though officially I'm still registered as a specially funded pianoforte soloist with Segismundo Alegría and the Vienna Philharmonic for the duration of the Estabrook Festival, Summer 1978. I know this is true, because one of my new Anarchist friends at the Black Orchid bar actually called the Festival offices to check me out; the secretary told him she wasn't allowed to comment on my musical competence, "if any," but I was in fact on record with them in what she called a "semi-active file"; and then she made some fantastic allusion to suicidal tendencies I was supposed to have. I don't know what to make of this last charge except to deny it straight out; the other insults are harder to answer, because I really do feel semi-active these days, and I'm not sure how I'd characterize my musical ability except to say that it's dubious and maybe even preterite; I suppose that's why I'm out here campaigning for the Anarchists right now instead of making music the way God meant me to.

I feel a little stupid trotting around Worcester this way for Zérault's mayoralty campaign, but I have to do something; I can't practice very well in this state of mind, and spending my time in the dormitory is not exactly my idea of entertainment. I have a feeling I'm never going to get asked to play in concert, and that's idiotic, because on my dresser I have a personal letter from Alegría inviting me to come to Estabrook this summer to do Beethoven's Third Piano Concerto—with the great man himself conducting!—and any musician worth his salt knows what that means to a person's career. When the letter arrived, I immediately packed up and came to Worcester on the bus. But ever since I got here, it's been total confusion. I'm ashamed to say that in all these weeks in residence I haven't even been able to find the main concert hall—and if Alegría is here, I'm certainly unaware of it. I haven't even heard a proper performance yet; all I do is go to an endless series of rehearsals, and every day it's a different piece, in a different hall, and always with people I have never seen before and who seem to have no particular interest in my skills or even in my name, though I must say they are unfailingly polite. Some of the conductors are just awful, but the musicians seem to be able to ignore them with a fair degree of success; I've even seen one beating time all alone on the stage, swooping and grimacing as if the orchestra had not left hours ago to catch the movie in town, and only I was left, occasionally playing a note or two at random out of a sense of propriety, but giving up at last and going home, or rather back to the dormitory and the inevitable chess game with Myksis, the Deutsche Grammophon representative for the Quinsigamond area, an eerie little Lithuanian with whom I share my modest quarters and who, at the moment, seems to be my only friend.

Last week I had a very unsettling experience at the Festival offices. I was determined to find out whether Alegría was really here and, if so, whether I could see him and perhaps get my career back on the track, and so one rainy day I marched into the main building and talked to a secretary named Eve, who told me what I had always been told on the phone—namely, that Dr. Alegría was indeed in residence but that his office hours varied and it was practically impossible to catch him.

Could I make an appointment, I asked?

No, appointments were not being made for this week.

For next week then?

No, I had to come back next week to make an appointment for next week.

I looked at her in desperate silence; her perfume was intoxicating, like a mixture of dust and sea salt. I tried to work on her sympathy by appearing helpless and childlike. But she stood up abruptly and told me I might as well save myself the trouble—since, as far as she was concerned, I was a dead man. I felt a surge of desire; she must have felt it too, because now she came around the desk and held my burning face in her hands and kissed me full on the mouth.

"Follow me," she whispered, and disappeared through a small door with a purple knob.

I followed immediately—I'm absolutely certain I went through the same door she did—but as it clicked shut behind me, I found myself in the alley in the drizzling rain, with no sign of Eve and no way to get back in except to go to the main entrance again and start over, which in my state of mind seemed like one da capo too many. So I went home in tears. Next time—if I ever do go back—I plan to march straight to the piano in Dr. Alegría's office and start to play, just to assert myself and my rights, like Zeitblom in the brothel (or was it his friend?). It will be a ridiculous gesture, I suppose, but I have nothing else left to do.

So here I am playing ward heeler, mostly out of boredom, canvassing the College Square area for the Anarchist ticket. We just might have a shot at the mayor's office this year with Théophile ("Big Ted") Zérault, the straw boss down at Ashland Steel, even though his only real campaign issue is that he wants to dismantle the Holy Cross conservatory and replace it with a facility of some more practical benefit to the community. Why I'm working for him I'm not really certain; I suspect myself of feeling some resentment toward the Holy Cross musicians, who have actually been able to perform at Estabrook while I sit on my hands. But there's more to it than that, of course. Anarchism has always seemed to be the only reasonable philosophy for a person like myself: as a musician, as a citizen, as a human being, I do not hesitate to admit that I am a political idiot, and my new friends at the Black Orchid—God knows—are quick to agree. At the same time, I think I have a right to know where I stand; for example, it seems a little strange to me that I've never met the candidate in all these months, considering that the Orchid is supposed to be his headquarters. I've never even heard a convincing physical description; I imagine him to myself as a huge, ruddy-faced, good-natured barbarian, somewhat jowly, with tinted glasses and a bulge in his jacket suggesting the presence of a pistol. This idea may be totally off the mark, but people have to make do with whatever images they can get when there's nothing else to go on—and, as far as I can tell, that's most of the time. I have to go through the most incredible mental gyrations just to make sense of my living arrangements, for instance, and that's one area of my life I would have expected to be able to understand.

I think I mentioned my roommate Myksis. We live in the suite that used to belong to old Professor Dervis, who died of chalk poisoning the month before we came and whose belongings were never properly cleared out, so that certain articles of his—an ornamental bowl with painted pheasants inside, a dog-headed cane of ash and steel, a Douay Bible bound in purple calf—have, by assimilation, become part of our ménage.

Myksis does all the cooking, since I have no talent in that area, and I suppose I should be grateful. But he always serves me breakfast in Dervis's old bowl, which I think may have something wrong with it because I've noticed a kind of purplish fluorescence in the oatmeal these past few mornings. While I have no reason to associate it with any intentions Myksis might have against me, I just thought I'd better mention it here in case anything happens to me and people wonder why.

There's something peculiar about the man: to begin with, I don't think his name is really Myksis at all, since he hardly ever looks up when I say it. His excuse is that he's a little deaf, which I'm afraid I don't believe, since one of his duties is supposed to be audio quality control in local recordings. Does that make sense if he's hard of hearing? —It does not! Learning about his supposed deafness has for some reason greatly increased my affection for him, and I'm terrified that my living arrangement, coupled with these irrational emotions, may be leading me to destruction—if not at breakfast, then in some other way too horrible to imagine; and soon, perhaps, very soon indeed. —But I'm sure I'm being unnecessarily hard on poor Myksis, who seems to be a good person underneath it all.

I've begun oversleeping almost every morning—from an obscure desire to miss rehearsal, I suppose—and then I open half an eye to find myself in the same indecipherable situation as the night before, with the little fellow shaking my arm and urging me to wake up in spite of my drowsy assertions that there is no waking, only different kinds of sleep.

At any rate, Myksis is my friend . . . perhaps not the kind of friend I would have wished for myself, but a friend nevertheless, and a good listener, and someone with whom I can share the intoxicating experience of Estabrook at the height of its season. They do some very interesting things here from time to time. Last summer, for instance, they staged what sounds like a really remarkable little piano piece of the experimental variety, and the Estabrook performance was the première, as I learned today from a scrapbook I found while going through some old papers of Dervis's. The piece was called *Fire with Fire!*, with no composer listed (though it seems the evening was made possible by a grant from the Worcester Anarchist Alliance). Judging from the description, it must have been one of the most expensive solo pieces ever created. According to Perdix, waxing purple for the *Worcester Telegram* Sunday music section, the piano had to be considered a total loss by the end of the concert. On a framework above the keyboard was suspended a large translucent container filled to the brim with superheated mercury, attached to a weighted steel rod and a central pivot, like a pendulum. The pianist's first duty, according to the score, was to break the membrane over a small hole at the bottom of the vessel and then to start it swinging, so that now and then a large drop of the heavy glowing liquid landed on a note, the weight of the metal being great enough to hold the key down until the enormous temperatures had fused it forever in a depressed position. Once this juggernaut was in operation, "to the delight and consternation of the adepts of St. Cecilia," the performer went behind the piano and mounted a platform supported by some dubious wooden staging; here he picked up a portable industrial laser in the shape of a thyrsos, which he waved at the audience in the obligatory fashion (Perdix: "the excitement was palpable"), then held it in front of him (in what was probably the only comfortable position) and began to beam it downward, severing the sounding wires one by one, two by two, or three by three. As each string broke, the audience was "convulsed with tremors as if the world were ending"; an A-flat, sounded and held by the burning mercury, would presently be obliterated by another A-flat of truly apocalyptic proportions but of almost no duration, since the strings that could have held it were gone; instead, all the remaining strings began to ring with a vengeance, "reminding the awed listener of a thousand mothers bewailing the death of as many sons."

I think the reviewer must have been correct in his judgment that "while certain neoclassical antecedents might be claimed for the piece," its "frank sexuality" and "anarchic Dionysian spontaneity" clearly linked it with the undergraduate tradition of piano-busting with sledgehammers. In any event, nothing like that has happened this summer—or if it has, we haven't heard about it;

we're supposed to get the *Telegram* every morning, but somebody always steals it. I wish there were some way to get accurate schedules. Maybe you have to be friends with some influential person . . . I just don't know.

If only I'd had the sense to go to Holy Cross in the first place!

I had the chance and let it slip, and now I think back on it with incredible longing, like a man who has lost certain rights forever.

You can see the campus from College Square—a great conglomeration of pillars, balconies, belfries, crenellations, and façades, all lined and banded with green copper, like a medieval city on a high hill. Between the buildings the very air seems to reverberate, and under the golden haze you can see banners and pennants of a hundred subtle colors. The young novices shuffle drowsily past me on their way to class; they seem to be ringed and wreathed in a splendid sleep, so that just to be near the rise and fall of their perfumed lungs is to know peace. I have never tried to speak to them as they pass, not even to hand them a leaflet. But I'm certain they would never answer or even notice they had been addressed: sleep fills their eyes like an unbroken membrane of belief. It seems infinitely touching that there should be people who spend their lives trying to wake them.

For some reason it's not possible—or not permitted—for persons like myself to visit Holy Cross. (It should be understood that this name refers exclusively to the conservatory; the rest of the school is something no one is able to believe in any longer. When a classicist or a historian tells me he's "teaching at Holy Cross this year," I have learned to understand it as an elegant euphemism for unemployment.) To begin with, it's far from certain whether the institution really is where it seems to be, in spite of the appearances I've just described. That seems incredible? —It did to me. So one day last week, deciding to see for myself, I borrowed Myksis's old Pontiac and drove through an ancient underpass to the other side of the Providence & Worcester tracks, where the buildings of Holy Cross shone for a moment in the sun before the roadside turned countrylike and green as if the entire city had been a dream. When I had passed the hill, I was surprised to find myself near the Black Orchid, which I had always approached from another direction. Now I took a sharp right into a residential area, thinking perhaps I could find an open gate at the back of the campus. But the road ended suddenly at the top of the hill near an old stone house that seemed empty and that, together with its extensive grounds, occupied the entire summit; in other words, it was in the exact spot where Holy Cross had appeared to be from the other side. On the great lawn, near the broken gazebo and the reflecting pool clogged with ash leaves, were several ornamental hen pheasants pecking disconsolately at the ground. There was not a soul in sight.

I had the feeling I'd seen the house somewhere before —indeed, when I had deciphered the name on the rusted steel plaque in the driveway, I recognized it as the backdrop for numerous family portraits I'd seen in Professor Dervis's scrapbook. The structure was huge and barren, with open doors everywhere, looking destroyed in spite of their wholeness, swinging in the breeze or banging helplessly against the jamb.

I parked the car by the nameplate and went inside.

The interior was a maze of oak and polished granite, with here and there a spiral staircase leading to the second floor. The odd thing was that there was no main stair. In fact, nothing in the house seemed to be principal. There was no door that was obviously a front door. No matter what side of the house you stood on, it seemed like the back. For a long time I tried to decide which room might have been the living room, because most of the cubicles had the dead air of cramped individual quarters.

In the pantry I found the skeleton of a servant—man or woman I couldn't tell. All at once I was overcome with desire, which in my experience is often released by an image of mortality, and I began pacing miserably up and down the corridors, not knowing what to do. Then, through a side window, I saw a young woman on the lawn, a recent widow, to judge from her dress; she was sitting on the remains of the summer house, reading a book bound in purple calf. I went out immediately and struck up a conversation—about what I don't remember.

She seemed to like me.

Her name was, of course, Eve.

After a decent interval, with the tender slowness of habitual lovers, we took off each other's clothes and sank together onto the grass.

People are so taken with what they see around them, so willing to believe! It never occurred to me to doubt the reality of the old stone house or the ruined gazebo, or the ornamental hen pheasants, even when the woman had dissolved into the grass in the very act of intercourse, or rather when I saw that she had never been anything but sweet clover and purple bluets like the rest of the cool green lawn on which I lay naked; and now the whistling of the wind began to sound strangely human and scornful, so that I ran awkwardly back to the car, pulling my clothes on as I went, and drove back the way I had come, wanting (I have to admit it)—wanting to die.

Just before the ancient underpass, I glanced up the hill, expecting to see the great house, but there was Holy Cross again, shining as bright as ever on the summit, and I realized, to my chagrin, that I had probably lain naked in human company I was unable to perceive, perhaps in the middle of a rehearsal, and the sounds I attributed to the wind may have been the jeering whistles of conservatory students whose practice had been comically interrupted by the lewdness of middle age.

I was surprised at this thought.

I think this was the day I began to doubt my sanity.

But I learned an important lesson when I saw the conservatory gleaming for the second time, impossibly, on the exact site of the ruined manor—namely, that an obsessive vision does not dissolve merely because it has been shown to be unreal.

My mood improved remarkably as I thought about this, and I was later able to practice a couple of hours without falling into the usual depression; I would even have gone to rehearsal, but by that time of course the secretaries had forgotten me completely, and I was never able to find out when my evening rehearsal was till the day after it was held, which was not really very useful.

I was never fitted for pure music, was always too clouded, too opaque. I used to think it was only an abundance of life—but on the day I searched for Holy Cross, I began to be afraid the life itself might be redundant and barren, a lonely inner city of whirling ash and freezing steel. It must have been this intuition of sterility that drove me to Anarchism, with its touching faith in human goodness. I confess I was not entirely uninfluenced by

A *Summer at Estabrook*

Zérault's hostility to the conservatory, especially after my difficult experience with it. He seems to have been some kind of avant-garde musician when he was young (he may even have studied composition with Alegría), but an ear infection put him out of action when he was still in his twenties, and ever since then he's hated all music with an unnatural passion, even to the point of being unable to trust anyone who can hold a tune. —It occurs to me that this may be the reason I've never met the great Théophile; our mutual friends must be keeping us apart, because Zérault has a violent temper, and if he walked into the Orchid when I was there he might go out of control and break my fingers, or whatever they do to discourage pianists in that part of town.

I wouldn't hold it against him. I suppose I even love him, though I'm terrified that he may be the instrument of my destruction—if not now, then soon, very soon. But basically he's a good person, and would most certainly make a good mayor—which is why I'm down in College Square right now, with Holy Cross looming above me like the City of God, trying to convince the good people of Worcester to vote for a man I've never met.

The comrades know I don't campaign very hard, but nobody at the Orchid seems to care—which is to be expected, since we Worcester Anarchists are not exactly famous for our political organization.

This evening I showed these speculations to Myksis, since, in spite of his despicable qualities and dubious identity, he continues to be my only friend. I instructed him to skip over the parts in which he was mentioned, insisting that they were the fruits of a casual paranoia and did not represent my real feelings.

"Très bien," he said absently, and settled down to the task in Dervis's old easy chair.

Myksis read somewhat dutifully at first—I began to collect the dirty coffee cups around the room so as not to appear to be watching—but later his interest must have increased, because I let a glass fall and break on the tile floor, and he didn't look up. I noticed him smiling unaccountably when he was about two-thirds of the way through, which made me very nervous. Then he grew more serious. When he'd finished, he slammed the manuscript down on the Formica and gave a loud whoop that made my blood run cold.

I looked at him as Schopenhauer's squirrel must have looked at the fatal snake, waiting for an explanation, even though I knew that any possible one would have to be infinitely destructive.

"It's marvelous!" he said. "I love it!"

I stood there like a stone. Of all the possible reactions this horrid little person might have had, this was the most unexpected.

"You love what?" I asked him finally, but was so extremely fearful of his answer that I bolted from the room before he had a chance to speak.

I ran down the street and under the railroad tracks all the way to the sanctuary of the Black Orchid, a good two miles, and didn't come home till past midnight. It's—wait a minute—it's one-fifteen—and even though I'm exhausted, I thought it might be a good idea to write these last notes before I went to sleep. I think I understand now why my very first reader (he's watching me as I write this) came so close to driving me insane with his incomprehensible praise.

My first thought was that he wanted to kill me, perhaps by driving me to a confused suicide on the tracks of the

A Summer at Estabrook

Providence & Worcester; then I reflected that, after all, we had been living together for several weeks in relative harmony and really were friends, at least in some extended sense of the word; it was unthinkable that he should wish to do me serious harm.

Then what could his enthusiasm mean?

An evening of serious drinking did not get me any closer to a solution, perhaps because I spent most of my time holding hands with a pretty French-Canadian girl in a low-cut purple dress.

She reminded me strongly of Eve, to the point that I even asked her name.

It was, of course, Eve.

I was going to see if I could convince her to come home with me when she dissolved without warning into the moonless night.

I finally staggered alone into the street, where the cold air sobered me a bit; ancient Chevrolets were oozing up and down the pavement like reptiles; to the north, far up on the hill, I could see the flashlights of the grave robbers moving back and forth on the grounds of the old stone mansion. It was then that I understood.

Myksis had read my work as though it were fiction!

I confess I have never in my life felt quite so frightened, or so alone.

The Family

Tomorrow is Thanksgiving, and they still haven't shown any signs of life. I think my brother must be up on the big hill again; my sister is probably with him as usual. Those two almost seem to live in the woods these days. It makes me nervous. My parents don't know what to do. They seem to think if they just look out the window long enough, the children will come home. But if they really want them to come, I think somebody's just going to have to go get them—namely, me.

I guess I could try to find them right now. I could take the woods road all the way up and look. If I don't actually spot them, I at least could hear them laughing, couldn't I?

It's an old dirt road that cuts off through the timber, leads partway up the big hill, and then comes back again

The Family

into my parents' garden. There are no lights up there. But it's impossible to get lost.

They're just there at the living-room window, dressed in dark colors, half in each other's arms. They're always rocking a little from side to side.

It's a lonely life. I can see why Thanksgiving is important to them. It's when the whole family is supposed to be together again.

I spend as much time with them as I can, though sometimes when we're in the front room the whole place seems too big to me and makes me feel like a dwarf. You think that's why my sister and brother stay so long in the woods?

I myself have always loved the house—not to mention the people in it! I like the great stone pillars, the clapboards, the lawn. The roof is made of slates, and they're always falling off. They could cut your head off if you were standing in the right place. And the insides are made for holidays.

Every year we have Thanksgiving dinner in the vaulted dining room in the back. It overlooks the garden. There's Dad's antique Persian carpet collection on the floors and the walls, and acres and acres of stained glass.

I can smell the turkey right now. It's everywhere.

I don't know how Mom does it.

All we have to do is get my brother and sister.

I think I'll go straight up. If they're not there, I can always come back. After all, tomorrow is Thanksgiving. Honest, I can already smell it.

Space Invaders

Sometimes in the heat of the summer, when there's nothing very interesting in the refrigerator and we're feeling housebound anyway, Nancy and I like to walk down to the Apollo to get something to eat and play the electronic games. Charlie doesn't cook too well, but he has a Space Invaders—our special addiction. So we try to get through whatever he puts on the plate, and then waste a few quarters on the machine after lunch. The neighbors smile tolerantly when they see us, as if they thought we were doing something infantile.

They're wrong. It's not a child's game.

Children play games with the idea of winning, and Space Invaders is not programmed to let you win. The point is simply to destroy as many of the enemy as possible before your own destruction is complete.

The game is fascinating, utterly different from the

Space Invaders

older generation of pinball machines with their familiar bells and lights and buzzers. At the drop of a coin, a battalion of lurid alien spacecraft appears in a pure blue heaven and begins firing killer rays at the planet below, defended only by yourself. You are equipped with three anti-spacecraft lasers, and your sole cover is a line of fragile green defense bases from between which you counterattack; these are quickly eroded, both by the barrage from above and by your own bad aim from below.

The battle is fought to the rhythm of a beating heart, slow and strong at first and then accelerating violently as the slaughter advances and the enemy's rage increases. If by luck you manage to destroy all the ships before your own guns are silenced or your bases overrun, the hostile fleet is suddenly resurrected in its entirety, and attacks you all over again.

This procedure turned out to be too much for old Professor Chase's nervous system, one day back in August of this year. We were in the Apollo having lunch as usual and saw him walking by looking lost, so we invited him in for a pizza and convinced him to try a round on the machine. He did brilliantly, knocking out all the threatening craft with his first laser. But when they regrouped and began firing again, he went to pieces right before our eyes, crying like a baby, the tears rolling down his cheeks so pathetically that Nancy and I each put an arm around him and led him sobbing back to the table, nearly toppling an elderly lady who had been watching the game over his shoulder. The machine, unopposed, overran his defenses in a series of deafening explosions. We hadn't expected such a reaction, though he'd warned us before he began that he was unaccustomed to stress and might do badly. In our enthusiasm, it seemed, we'd provoked a crisis of some kind, and we felt guilty. I thought perhaps we'd disoriented him by pulling him too far out of his usual orbit, which was not easy for him but was at least familiar: sparsely attended classes on the Elizabethan poets, a lonely bachelor apartment, endless negotiations with abrasive young deans who wanted him to retire.

"It's not your fault," he said finally. "I'm afraid I've embarrassed you with this scandalous performance."

"Don't worry about us," I said, patting his arm. "How are you doing?"

He hesitated, as if about to say something important, then reconsidered and took a long drink from an Orange Fanta can left over from lunch. "I had understood that when I wiped out the enemy, the game was won," he said.

"It sets up again," said Nancy.

He looked better now, smiling a little ruefully as he gazed through the plate-glass window into the merciless glare of the treeless street. The elderly woman was leaving; I thought I recognized her as one of the secretaries from the university. He followed her with his eyes until she was gone.

"That was Betty," he said. "A wonderful woman."

We sat in silence.

"And I believed I'd won," he said.

"The game is stacked against you," I told him. "Your defenses are limited, and the number of enemy ships is infinite. You can't win; you just play."

"You ought to publish that idea," said Chase. "It might help your chances for tenure."

"Maybe that's why it's so fascinating," I went on. "You should see what it's like at Worcester Center. As soon as you run out of quarters, the next person in line pushes you out of the way so he can get started. And everybody loses! People seem to be playing in order to lose."

"I played to win," he said.

There were tears in his eyes again.

I remembered being told by one of his junior colleagues that Professor Chase was already in his second childhood, and should have the grace to step down and let a younger man have a try. The remark had struck me as cruel and self-serving, since the man who made it was up for tenure and would certainly get it if Chase's salary line were vacated through an early retirement.

To me, up to this moment at least, the old man had always seemed witty and sane. Now he couldn't hold back his tears no matter how he tried.

He stuttered an apology and got up to leave. Nancy and I followed him—we couldn't send him home alone in this condition—and walked him slowly back to his apartment on Woodland, some three blocks away.

The woman he had called Betty, surely one of the secretaries in the English Department, was waiting on the porch when we arrived. The professor fell into her arms.

"You poor, poor dear," she said, stroking his gray hair smooth as he crumpled against her. "How could the committee do that to you? They had no right!" Then we were all crying like children in spite of ourselves, and the game seemed very far away.

Scherzo with TV Antenna

Oh, Tony, even up here in the attic I could never see over the hills to Concord where you are, not even if the sun was up. But I imagine it all the time, and how it would be to be with you constantly instead of just once in a while on visiting days. I love to think of your face growing younger, the way it went from middle age back to childhood in those incredible weeks when I was really with you. But I understood, and I still do, and I still love you.

My parents both think I slept with you and they figure that's why your wife left you and you had to go to the hospital. They've got it totally backwards, as usual. They think of me as a home-wrecker. They haven't really smiled at me once for three years. Oh, come on, sure they have; most of the time they forget. But when the conversation ever does get around to that May they always

Scherzo with TV Antenna

say the same thing and I tell them it's not true and they just look depressed as if to say, our daughter is a liar.

That's one of the reasons I'm so sad around here. I spend huge amounts of time in the attic, like now, in this room with the TV antenna my dad was too special to put on the roof like everybody else. He doesn't want the neighbors to know the Underwoods have television. I think of you all the time up here.

I love looking down from this window in the daytime—here and there there's a hole in the treetops so I can see parts of the yard, the hedge between our property and Mrs. Katz's that I'm supposed to keep trimmed but I hardly ever do, Mrs. Katz's little fishpond with the green glass ball on its cement stand, the violet beds that always seem to have at least one cat fooling in them, the flagstone path that the milkman ought to be coming up in about two hours—I wonder if I was naked whether he'd look up or whether he'd just go back and forth as if I was invisible. But it's too cold to try it. This is one of the reasons I think it wouldn't be too good to write this all down, because if my parents ever read it I'd really be in trouble. It's better just to think it.

I remember when they talked about Eden in Sunday school and I always imagined me as God in this window looking down on my garden, imagining things that were not all that good going on under the trees where I couldn't see through the big leaves, like people eating a certain forbidden apple and then being banished across the hedge to the green globe and the fishpond and Mrs. Katz and the rest of those mysterious peoples of the earth. Except that I always made one change in the story, which was to let Adam apologize.

"Why did you do it?" I'd boom out from my great tall window as the sun rose and the angel let Adam in again just for a minute to state his case. "Why did you eat the apple?"

Anyway, I think it's fascinating how when you're asked to imagine a garden you always pick a real garden you know, instead of making up a new one. I think you could probably figure out a lot about people if you could only get them to admit the particular places they were imagining when they were supposed to be just thinking in general.

In these early hours before the sun comes up I always think about problems that don't seem to have answers, and the main one that keeps coming back is about sleep and what it has to do with my personality. Back in that spring when you were well, you used to say dreaming was the most important thing in my eyes. Naturally, I had to go and try that one out on Mr. Kearney, my guitar teacher. Without mentioning you by name, of course. He said he didn't know about my eyes.

I'm wide awake and the sleep is all outside in the air.

Are you listening? Where are you, Tony, dearest Tonio? I guess I forgot you for a minute. I just need to tell you things. I'll write you a real letter someday, but for now we'll just talk, okay?

Did you ever swim underwater on a breezy day and look up through the surface at the sky? That way the sun is like a fish swimming in the air. It's like a goldfish. When you were here, you were like a diver moving toward a breathing place, but you just plain drowned before you got there. Back when you were okay, you said you loved my emptiness. Remember how I got about it? But if I was really empty like you said, why didn't you come and fill me up?

The one time we tried you couldn't. Then look what happened, you nearly killed me.

Scherzo with TV Antenna

I'm not angry now. Don't worry. I'm just very sad.

It's so dusty in here, and there's no room to move. What if I just let myself fall out onto the driveway? But then I'd miss the sunrise. Anyway, it shouldn't be called that, all it is is my own planet going around and around. The sun just sits there.

Anyhow, all of us are supposedly traveling through space at enormous speeds, maybe into a black hole somewhere.

Oh, God, Tony, this antenna is so huge, it fills the room. Why couldn't he put it on the roof like everyone else?

Is that the morning star (which is really Venus) or a man-made satellite?

I don't think it's moving.

My dad would find me on the driveway, all withered up.

I bet you wonder why I'm at home. Well, sometimes I just get so sick of life with people.

Take Freddie, for example. He was the third and last date of my freshman year—totally, totally my parents' idea. I had my friends from high school, for God's sake, it's not as if I was in a strange town. But they have their ideas and I have mine. Freddie was the son of a classmate of my dad's who had a bakery in Bellows Falls, and naturally his father sent him to the old alma mater so he could learn the drinking songs, etc. I don't mean to be too hard on that place. It has its good points, I guess. I know I personally have had some really exciting courses. On the other hand, I'd like to know if it's so great, how come everybody has to get drunk all the time?

Anyway, Freddie took me out and talked my ear off about the ideals of his fraternity. I guess he hadn't asked around, so he didn't know he was third man up and the first two had struck out, one in a car and the other in a bathroom. I'm sure this would sound gross to an outsider. You just have to know how it was around there. He was drunk as a fish by the time we left the party. But he looked like a fish to begin with, which is why the comparison sounds so perfect. He was really disgusting. So here we are outside, supposedly walking me home, and he right away starts trying to hump me.

Christ, I was so desperate after my freshman year that I got in with a bunch of zombies and spent practically the whole summer stoned out of my mind. So everybody started saying I was totally "out of reach." At least, that's what my mother kept saying. And they had these ministers and counselors and psychologists running all over the place trying to pull me out of it.

When September rolled around, I just got sick of the whole thing, all on my own, and it was over.

I mean, I still smoke now and then, but nothing like that summer. I got out of it for the same reason I got into it. From boredom.

You're the only person I ever loved, Tony. Maybe it's because you're the only person more self-centered than I am.

Don't get offended. It's just true, that's all.

The first time I saw you without clothes on, it was a real shock. I mean, there was nothing *wrong* with you. But you were so *slight*—and I couldn't help wondering why I'd never seen it before.

I think it's because when you were teaching you used to swagger a lot, which made you seem bigger. And there was all that tweed to fill you out. And your hearty voice. You're actually a little taller than Kearney, I think—but

Scherzo with TV Antenna

he seems a lot taller because he's so solid, and he stands straight. He never stoops or hangs his head the way you do.

Well, you *do*—I'm sorry.

Of course, he's older than you by about ten years, and that makes a difference.

Also, I think you seem slighter because you're so blond and fair-skinned and your bones are so delicate. Next to you, Kearney would look like a giant.

Remember when I thought I was in love with him?

That was so embarrassing.

I was at a lesson one Saturday, about a month after you left—I was practicing like crazy in those days. Just to keep busy, of course. Anyway, that's when I told him.

Sometimes I feel like an only child, you know? My brother and sister seem really unreal, as if there had always been a glass wall between me and them. It didn't help that when my brother was born he looked like a snake. He had that look. And my sister was just plain ugly from the beginning. Also, she doesn't seem to have any character at all that I can see.

Though I should talk! Who knows how much I have?

But at least I play an instrument.

No kidding, it feels to me as if there's just me and my parents. I know they always thought I was both the smart one and the cute one, which is pretty good. Usually, the smart one is ugly and the cute one is dumb, and here they were the same person, me.

But it's hard to judge objectively about yourself. I could see how certain things I do could be seen as cute, though I'd never plan it that way. I'm just what I am, that's all.

I wonder if the apple blossoms down there can smell themselves? I mean, if birds can see about two hundred more colors than we can, maybe flowers have senses we never even heard of.

I remember I said something like that in the very first paper I ever handed in to you, and it came back with some zany remarks about *pantheism* and *sentimentality* and the fact that you didn't *like* it.

Thanks a bunch.

I don't think for a girl my age it was all that bad. You just have to realize you were judging my work by an older person's standards.

That January was weird, you know? I suddenly got this fix on you as an adult. I mean really *old*. But you were pretty cute, actually.

Imagine, my parents think I caused the whole thing. But it was really your wife, right?

Do you know how much you told me? I bet you have no idea. We used to have these fabulous talks together. Do you remember? Is all this just totally erased from your mind now?

That's really scary if it is.

Those were the most incredible times I ever spent in my entire life! The talks, I mean—the two of us naked and talking.

Oh, Tony, you were so silly sometimes!

Hey, look at me, teaching the teacher.

Listen, honey, I'm sorry to fall into this tone of voice, but it makes me so mad to think what a waste it was. Everybody said you were so bright. I mean, of course you were. But it was important that they knew it, too.

Everybody knew about us, you know?

There's one thing I want to tell you, which is how I felt when I woke up in the hospital and you were there. You looked terrible, but *you were there*. And somehow

Scherzo with TV Antenna

you'd gotten *me* there, which was good because it was possible I had a slight concussion and anyway they had to take a few stitches in my head.

Maybe they should have taken a few more, come to think of it.

But I don't blame you for what you did. Hey, I made you. I know that. Believe me, Tony darling, you just did what I made you do.

It's getting gray out. It's like little dots of dark and light out there that you can't really fit together with your eye.

I'm smiling now, just thinking about you. My dad should be up here. He loves it when I smile. That means I can make him love me whenever I want.

You said you loved my emptiness.

Are you there, Tony?

What ever happened to the birds? Maybe it's not as late as I thought.

It takes too long! How many hours could I have been sitting here, anyway?

My legs are all cramped up. I can hardly move anyway in this place.

The Claims Adjuster

I was hoping to get some work done at home last Saturday, but it was so hot in the house and the kids were so impossible that I scrapped that plan and went for a long walk up in Green Hill Park. I felt guilty, because we need all the extra money we can get now that we're saddled with this huge house. But I can't spend my whole life dealing with people who buy a policy and then expect you to pay off every time they break a fingernail. I need some rest. I've been working much too hard lately, and I resent it when I end up having more responsibilities in my free time than I have during the week, because somehow, somewhere, a person has to relax.

It isn't just the work, either. There's always the pressure to get involved in the community—church fairs, Boy Scouts, Rotary, you name it—which is fine in principle but never seems to leave you any time for yourself.

The Claims Adjuster

For instance, I got roped into the Big Brother program a few years ago when the people at the head office decided our image needed some burnishing, and I didn't mind it at first, I even felt I might be helping those kids find their way in the world—they were Indian children, from the reservation out in Grafton. But it got to be very emotionally draining, and after a few months I decided I'd better just tend to business and let the world take care of its own problems. The tribal elders seemed to take it as a personal insult when I told them I was pulling out, which I thought was totally uncalled for, since they knew from the beginning I was there on a volunteer basis. We still support the program with financial contributions, so I think we have all the visibility we need in that area; and what I personally need, as I told my boss, is a peaceful weekend now and then so I can come back on Monday morning and do my job right—and I see my bad experience on Saturday as just one more indicator of how stressful the job can be. I'll explain what happened; you can judge for yourself.

I drove the old Pontiac up Belmont Street, parked by the insane asylum, and started up the access road on foot. People were golfing off to the right, and some joggers went bouncing by on the dry gravel, looking pale and tired. I had a splitting headache and some disorientation, symptoms my doctor says may be related to a hereditary condition (but which could just as well be due to overwork, in my opinion); what bothered me most was the unpleasant floating sensation I always get when I take time out for no particular reason, probably because, deep down, I still believe in the old saw that time is money. But I kept right on walking, because I don't like the idea that work is my only ballast in this world. My face suddenly began to itch; I discovered I'd forgotten to shave and there was heavy stubble on my chin. I must have looked like a felon.

At the park entrance, I stopped to rest and read the collection of signs that tell you what to expect inside. It was an idle exercise; most of these attractions, as I'd learned on my last visit, are nowhere to be found. I imagine ANIMAL FARM could refer to the half-dozen sheep and goats that live out behind the pagoda, and ASTRO CITY must be the aluminum rocket ship down by the lake, but INDIAN CAMP and BUFFALO PEN are clear cases of false advertising, just like the plaque underneath them that was put up to celebrate THE 300TH ANNIVERSARY OF THE BEHEADING OF MATOONUS, CHIEF OF THE NIPMUCS.

Now I happen to know a little something about King Philip's War, and the idea that Matoonus was beheaded here in Worcester is definitely an invention of the Chamber of Commerce (it was on Boston Common). It's always the same, whether it's a matter of a scratched bumper or water damage to interior walls or something as big as the history of a nation; the simple fact is that people lie a lot. I had the uncomfortable feeling I was working again, but I couldn't help it. When I see fraud of any kind my blood begins to boil.

As I was reading the signs, a guard came out of the bushes and asked for my name. Something about him seemed familiar; he was dark and short and kept wiping his hands compulsively on his trousers. From the complete absence of facial hair, at first I thought he must be a child, then that he must belong to another race.

"Calvin Gill," I said.

He wrote it laboriously in his notebook and sat down on the ground under BUFFALO PEN.

The Claims Adjuster

On an impulse I asked him whether there really were buffalo somewhere in the park, since I'd never seen a live one and would have been very interested.

"Bloody murder," he said quietly, making little sworls in the dirt with his finger.

I started in surprise, but from the disjointed grin on his face as he spoke I finally realized he wasn't a guard at all but one of the harmless outpatients from the asylum, out for his afternoon stroll and playing a little game with one of the saner members of society. Now he wasn't smiling anymore, and his face grew tense and angry.

"Wash it off!" he shouted. "Wash it off!"

Having no idea what he meant, and not particularly interested in finding out, I waved goodbye and walked on into the park.

As I rounded the first curve, where the woods give way to the open land, I saw my day wasn't going to be as private as I'd thought. A crowd had gathered around a few folksingers on a makeshift wooden platform, and I learned from a cheaply printed flyer that it was an Indian benefit concert. The music had already begun; I found myself in the middle of the audience as people closed in behind me, and before long someone was passing the hat for the Wampanoag Legal Fund. That got me angry, because I think that issue is the single most idiotic thing to come before the American courts in the last two hundred years.

When I refused to make a donation, patiently explaining my reasons, some of the younger "Native Americans" (as they like to call themselves) began to act as if they wanted my scalp, pushing me back and forth and calling me a thief and a dog and I don't know what else; it was very unpleasant. The star performer stopped in mid-song and glared down at me like an angry schoolmarm. A hush fell over the crowd.

"Welcome, little brother," she said, in what I thought was a very insulting tone. "Do I understand correctly that you're opposed to the land claims of the Wampanoags?"

"I most certainly am," I said, sure of my ground in spite of the hostile looks I was getting from everyone around me. I was determined not to lose my head.

"And why is that?" this creature said with exaggerated politeness.

My family had recently been unable to sell their cottage on the Cape because of the preposterous claims of the so-called Wampanoag tribe (which is not legally a tribe at all). I went to the heart of the matter.

"What you don't seem to know," I said in a loud clear voice so that everyone could hear, "is that the idea of private property is totally alien to Indian tradition. You started off saying it was wrong to own land, and now hundreds of years later you say you want it back. It's hypocritical, and it's extremely unfair."

I had not finished, but this personage began another of her songs to drown me out, something about the buffalo being gone, and I found myself surrounded by a tight cordon of concert marshals, who proceeded to escort me, through a gauntlet of insults, to the periphery of the crowd. With a feeling of disgust, but proud that I'd at least presented my opinions forcefully, I turned my back on them all and struck out across the open grass toward the top of the hill.

High on the forward slope, the military had marked off an area for maneuvers. There's an army base of some kind on the access road, but this was the first time I'd seen them invade civilian territory, and I wondered whether it was strictly legal. I thought not. Some foreign-

The Claims Adjuster

looking black soldiers were practicing hand-to-hand combat, led by a white U.S. Marine sergeant, and I deduced that I was watching some of the Haitians who are here in Worcester by special arrangement with the Defense Department, for counter-insurgency training, or some such nonsense. I'd met a few of them in a Worcester bar, and I remember being impressed by the immaculate Parisian they spoke among themselves, not to mention the perfect English they used with me. (Our own Haitian community seems to avoid them, probably out of a sense of cultural inferiority.) It was impossible to tell whether I knew any of the soldiers I was seeing today, and not only because of their distance from me but because—all racist clichés aside—their jet-black complexions and striking Negroid features really do make it extremely difficult to tell one individual from another. I had had a similar experience with my little Indian brothers in Grafton—I kept mixing up their names—and it was hard to make the responsible members of the tribe understand that a keen sensitivity to racial characteristics does not, in itself, constitute racism.

The day was blue and vast. I let my vision swing wide, over the steaming city and the hills and forests beyond, breathing freely and feeling much better in spite of the recent unpleasantness. A huge St. Bernard was trotting around the soldiers like a mascot; as I passed the group at a distance, the dog began to gallop toward me, barking so deep and strong that the ground seemed to shake under my feet. I kept walking as calmly as I could, thinking that if he threatened to attack me I'd stand with my legs together and my hands clasped on my chest, a trick that sometimes confuses these animals. But by the time the beast arrived, I saw he meant to be friendly, and we went on up the hill together toward a kind of stone altar on the crest, the dog running in great circles around me, barking at things like butterflies as if to tell me not to worry. I reached the altar, an odd construction surrounded by sweet fern and broken bottles, and stopped to rest.

Now I heard the sergeant bellowing in my direction. But when I turned in surprise, I judged that what I'd taken to be my name was in fact a military command, and the Haitian irregulars, divided into pairs, were going through the motions of cutting each other's throats with long field knives. The dog began acting strangely, making hooing noises and moving backwards somewhat as he nuzzled the grass with his face, first one side and then the other. There was something sexual in his movements; they reminded me of ritual courtship dances I'd seen in wildlife films. It made me nervous. Not knowing what else to do, I walked on over the brow of the hill. Now I could look down on the northern curve of the interstate and see my employer of twenty years, the Mutual Assurance Company of America, glowing yellow and pearl in the declining sun.

Then something happened that I'm not sure how to describe; I've tried again and again to explain it to myself, and it still makes no sense. The ground simply went out from under my feet. There was no dog and no insurance company. Everything went black as pitch, and the world seemed to be smothering in a pillow of silence. For a time I heard my heart beating as if at a great distance. Then the dog reappeared far off in a gray mist, enormous and frightful now, his eyes red moons and his body dark satin. He opened his mouth, full of luminous teeth, and by their light I could see thousands of men and women of all races falling from every corner of the sky down through air thick with copper coins, so thick I could hardly breathe.

It was then that I lost consciousness.

Near evening, I was awakened by the odor of sweet fern, feeling damp and stiff as if I'd spent the night on a forest floor. I sat up and rubbed my eyes. The sun was setting. Far down in the valley, the Mutual Assurance Company was in shadow, the entrance bathed in automatic emergency lights. Whatever had happened to me, it was over.

I started for home, whistling a little to reassure myself, but the landscape acted strangely on my anxiety, and for a moment I imagined that the setting sun was Matoonus's head, severed horribly and dripping gore as it stared blindly out across what had become, suddenly, a foreign country.

Other soldiers were in training now, a Haitian sergeant instructing a group of sour-faced Hispanics. On the word *kill*, they lunged at each other with an enthusiasm that seemed almost sexual. I sat down again to watch. After a time, I saw the dog loping toward me, barking softly as if he had recovered a friend.

Together, we walked toward the gate in the massing darkness. The houses hung like lanterns on the far slopes of the city, and a cool breeze began to clear the air. The concertgoers were nowhere to be seen. When we reached the entrance, now brilliant with fluorescent light, I noticed the mental patient I'd met on the way in was still sitting under the signs. It was far too late for him to be here. As I went by, nodding uncomfortably in his direction, something in his expression stopped me cold.

"Robbie!" I cried, forgetting my anguish in the surprise of the moment. He grinned insanely, wiping his fingers nervously on the sleeves of his jacket.

I had recognized him, after all.

Robbie—the Americanized version of his name—had been one of my little brothers in the Grafton days, a Nipmuc child who'd been orphaned in unspeakable circumstances. I felt I'd developed a special rapport with him, but he was depressive and difficult, as one would expect; his problems had quickly grown too severe for a layman to handle, and I'd had to stand by helplessly as he was taken out of school and sent to the Belmont Home for psychiatric treatment. (He suffered from the delusion that everything in the world was covered with blood.) I'd forgotten about him completely in the intervening years, and I was sad to find his condition hadn't improved.

"You Gill!" I think he said. His enunciation had never been very good.

"It's time to go home, Robbie."

"No, no, no!"

He was as difficult as ever. "Yes, it is," I said. "The nurses will be wondering where you are, and you wouldn't want them to worry, would you?"

"*I'm not Robbie!*" he said angrily.

He wasn't?

No, of course he wasn't! It was the other boy, the one I'd always confused with Robbie because their problems had been so similar. Was he in the Home too? I had no idea, and couldn't think of a way to ask him discreetly. Instead, I smiled broadly as if the whole thing had been a joke, inquiring how he was in the most cautious and general terms, because, for the life of me, I still couldn't remember his name.

The fellow had taken hold of my sleeve, jabbering

words I didn't understand. In spite of my explanations that it was late and I had to be going, there seemed to be no way to escape him without the use of force. The dog began to growl as if to defend me. But I barked a command, and it sat down obediently.

Lifting the boy by the armpits, I swung his legs out from under him and dropped him back onto the ground, where he crumpled into a fetal position, staring up at me like the bewildered savage he was. Warning him that he was going to have to be more civil in his actions if he expected the world to take him seriously, and promising to look him up sometime soon, I left for home with the dog at my heel.

In retrospect, it seems strange that the St. Bernard should have come home with me, though at the time it seemed perfectly natural. On my way down the access road, as I listened to the huge animal striding beside me in the darkness with his heavy padding footsteps and cavernous breathing, all I could think of was how expensive it would be to feed such a beast.

Need I say my fears have turned out to be more than justified?

We still don't know who the dog belongs to. Maybe by now he belongs to us—he certainly had no qualms about adopting me—but I'm sure someone, somewhere, must think he's in the hands of a thief.

Freedom

My brother-in-law Danny is not a happy person these days. He spends his life looking for the big score, which never comes, and in the meantime he sits around the house driving us crazy. He and my sister Hallie moved in with me last May, when his unemployment checks ran out. I was living alone in a big house; what could I say? I could have told them Danny drinks too much. But they knew that already.

He got arrested a while ago. It was a Friday around the middle of July. Danny had been at it all afternoon, and by dinnertime he was nearly out of control. I watched him lose a big gob of spaghetti into his lap; first he mopped it with a napkin, and when that didn't work, he brushed it all onto the floor. My sister told him to cut it out.

He said he was sorry.

Freedom

She got a paper towel and began to clean up the mess. "I'll tell you one thing, Danny," she said, "you're not going out tonight."

"I've got to," he said, rocking back and forth over his plate. "I have to do the deal with Shaughnessy I told you about. Do you know what that means, honey? It means we can move out of here for good. Wouldn't you like that?"

She shook her head. "Please stay home," she said.

Nobody spoke for a while. It was hot in the kitchen. We had the windows wide open, but there was no breeze at all.

"There's a job at the lumber outlet," I told Danny. "Why don't you get some sleep and talk to Harrison in the morning?"

He looked at me, boozy and resentful. "Listen, Dave, if you're worried about the money, I can pay you back every cent we've cost you up to now—with interest."

"You don't owe me anything," I said.

"I don't?" Danny said. "Who says I don't!"

"Don't get so offended," said Hallie. "He says we don't owe him anything."

"But I am offended," Danny said.

"Maybe you could use a drink," I told him.

Hallie groaned.

"That's very funny," Danny said. "That's the kind of funny goddamn remark I could never come up with."

"Oh, stop it," Hallie said.

"No," Danny said, "that's really goddamn funny, him with his house and his car—"

"I worked hard for these things," I said.

"And he's also putting a roof over our heads," said Hallie.

"All I'm trying to say," Danny said, "is how much I admire your brother, honey. What's wrong with that?" He leaned back dangerously in his chair. "Hell," he said, "I'm just crazy about the little goddamn pansy."

"I'm going down in the field for a while," I told Hallie.

"Don't you walk away from me!" Danny shouted.

"Danny, please don't," said Hallie. "Tell Dave you're sorry."

He turned angrily to face her. But he couldn't think of anything to say. As I reached the back yard, he called out the window that he was sorry.

"It's okay," I said.

I don't know if he heard me. I didn't care.

Sunset had come and gone. I sat on the far side of the pond, watching the lights on the water. Up on the hill, the house looked sullen. I decided to sell it first chance.

Hallie found me there.

"The police just called," she said. "Danny's been arrested for drunk driving. Will you go with me to get him? I'm scared."

"Relax," I told her. "It's nice and cool here. We have plenty of time."

"How can you say that?" she said.

"He's not going anywhere," I said.

"So you're not coming?"

"No," I said. "The law is the law, and he'll just have to understand that."

There was a long silence. Carp were jumping in the water, leaving ripples the moon caught. I was getting drowsy, or something.

"Do you think I should divorce him?" she said.

Freedom

I didn't say anything.

She stood up, stretching.

"Come on," she said. "It was your car he was driving."

The station was airless and hot. We sat by the dispatcher's desk for an hour, waiting for the chief to come. He never did. I later learned that Danny had threatened to kill the man.

The bail commissioner was a heavyset woman in her forties. She installed herself behind a large table in the inner office; a police sergeant brought the prisoner in and maneuvered him into a chair. Danny was still very drunk.

"Thanks for coming down," he told us. "I'm really sorry. I don't even know what happened."

"Sign this, please," said the commissioner.

Danny did. She gave him the carbon copy.

"Your bail is two hundred dollars," she said. "You don't have to pay it. If you fail to appear at the arraignment Monday morning, a warrant will go out for your arrest and you'll be liable for the full amount. You owe me fifteen dollars bail fee, and then you're free to go. Do you agree to these conditions?"

"No!" Danny moaned, gesturing helplessly. "Two hundred dollars! Christ!"

"Did you understand what the lady said?" the cop asked him.

"I'm not going to pay no two hundred dollars, that's all I know," Danny said. "This is a free country."

I took out fifteen dollars and gave the money to the woman.

On the way to the door, Danny had a thought. He pulled away from us and went back.

"I want something that shows I paid," he said.

We waited. They looked so tired in there.

"Sir," said the commissioner. "We don't give receipts. Your freedom is your receipt."

"Like hell it is!" Danny said. "I want something the hell written down!"

The Teacher

The following is the story of William Hunter and his mistress Bange Tage, recorded here by a man who loved them both.

William Hunter—whom I think I may refer to as my disciple—was a Boston University musicologist who went to Central America on a research grant in the fall of 1979, some months after the Sandinist victory in Nicaragua, when that country was trying to reestablish the rhythm of its national life and El Salvador and Guatemala were still laboring under the weight of their respective dictatorships. In less than six months he was dead, cut down by a counter-insurgency unit of the Guatemalan army on a grassy road in the hills near Quezaltenango. His family would like the world to believe that he was innocently collecting musicological data when he got

The Teacher

caught in a crossfire; the simple fact, which everyone must know by now, is that he died fighting for the revolution.

Bange Tage, the woman he loved, came to this country from Munich in 1973. At the time Hunter met her, she was working at a community service agency in the South End. (She was also a night student of mine.) Physically, nothing could have been further from the Aryan ideal: the woman was small, sensual, and perfect, with thick brown hair and endlessly deep dark eyes. Intellectually, she ran to extremes that were perhaps Germanic. For five years she was Hunter's mistress; they had a son together (the boy Rudolph, now 3). She is, or was, a dedicated Communist revolutionary, and was fighting beside William when he died. The name Bange Tage is a pseudonym. Beyond that—to my embarrassment, since I've had excellent opportunities for observation—I know almost nothing about the woman, except that in some sense she led my dear Hunter to his death.

I am not the kind of person who ordinarily engages in political controversy, but in this case I've been so deeply involved from the beginning that I really have no choice. Hunter was by far the best graduate student I've ever had at Harvard, and my loyalty to his memory forces me to put down the truth exactly as I understand it, since it's obvious he would not have exposed himself to such risk if he had not wanted his actions to have some effect on the conscience of the world. The manner of his life and death in Guatemala is an implicit challenge to America's suicidal policy of supporting dictators in the Third World, and while it's clear that his extremism was inadmissibly romantic as a political posture, I would be glad if a certain number of people were moved sufficiently by his story to pressure this government into withdrawing support from tyrannical régimes like Lucas García's and encouraging the growth of liberal democracy wherever possible; then we could say with confidence that he did not die in vain.

I confess I'm a little worried over what his parents may decide to do once these revelations are public property. I've known old Professor Hunter since graduate school, and I must say I never really knew the meaning of vindictiveness until I took his seminar on Palestrina. His wife is just as bad. To this day they haven't so much as agreed to visit their own grandchild, though they have their little stratagems for seeing him anyway; more than one fine Sunday I've seen them walk past Bange and Rudi on the Cambridge Common, cutting her dead as they devour the child with their eyes. Bange practically goes to pieces when they do this (as they well know). When she got back from Guatemala, I told her to expect a custody suit from the grandparents within a few days, so she called a lawyer and waited. But nothing happened. It was almost as if the senior Hunters were afraid (of what?). Now, as the months go by, it seems less and less likely that they'll take any action (apart from more harassment), but it's always an annoying possibility. Who could ever convince them to love poor Bange, the agent (as they surely see it) of their son's destruction?

And in strictly rational terms, it would be difficult to argue with that description of her. She certainly had a hand in politicizing William, and of course it was Bange's contacts in the Party in Guatemala that made William's adventure possible at all. Before they knew each other, he had always described himself as apolitical, whatever that means. But if he was as apathetic as he seemed to believe he was, how would he have explained the intoxicating effect Bange's politics had on him from the moment he met her?

The Teacher

I do remember William getting upset in my seminar on the Vienna School (my only foray so far into the twentieth century) when he felt that the politically committed Eisler had been slighted in favor of Berg and Webern; in general, though, he shared my inclination to pure music. We remained close in the years following his doctoral studies—I was responsible for his appointment at B.U. under Dello Joio—and it did not bother me particularly to see his tastes moving toward the left, since I realized that an intellect can tire even of the most exquisite abstractions and begin to long for something with the odor of life upon it. It followed from this that when he told me he wanted to go on this musico-anthropological jaunt of his, I not only did not oppose the idea but actively encouraged it, writing the necessary recommendations on William's behalf and calling old friends and colleagues connected with the OAS, thinking (I suppose) that the fellow would get it out of his system that way. I knew the grant would be automatic, since his credentials —linguistic as well as musical—were impeccable.

But at that time, of course, I had no idea Bange would be going too.

It should not really have surprised me, since Hunter had been visibly dependent on her almost from the very day he met her. (It was in my office in the spring of '74; she was taking an extension course in harmony with me and we had become rather close.) His first reaction to her was spectacular and profound, as my own had been. In those days, she still had an aggressively virginal quality about her—though of course Bange was not physically a virgin—, a kind of delicious greenness that set a man's teeth on edge and made his heart leap, her eyes full of luscious violence, nervous and sensual, her body like a perfect fugue. She would begin to overflow with her own thoughts—that is, with visions of the revolution—and check herself suddenly with an affecting twitch of her generous lips, pursing them a little as if to say: *I'm not letting down my guard*, and then she'd get up her nerve anyway and let you have it with both barrels. I think it was this courage in the attack that was Bange's most attractive characteristic, and William admired it so much that sometimes I wonder whether he was not drawn to her through an obscure desire for personal destruction. I know how he felt, because I myself was often under fire, and I experienced the same seductive, debilitating enchantment every time. One afternoon in William's presence she called me a disgusting bourgeois snob, and told me I should be strangled in my sleep for living the life I led—and before I could react, she gave me a smile so dazzling and sexual it made my head reel and my knees go weak, so that I couldn't seem to say anything and just sat there stupidly, trying to ride it out, no longer understanding or caring where the joke ended and her rage began.

William just laughed.

When I later learned they had become lovers—though I had expected they would—my feelings were divided. Two people I cared for were making each other happy: what more could I ask? And still, and still. I suppose I was jealous. From then on I never could see them together without feeling some degree of annoyance (which I admit was irrational and unjustified). William immediately picked up her Marxist vocabulary, but used it—I thought—always with an edge of humor, as if it were only an ironic gesture of his in response to Bange's extravagant mannerisms. Later, he started to take some of

The Teacher

the jargon seriously, and that was when his troubles began.

It was plain to his friends that political events in Central America in the middle and late seventies had also had a profound effect on his thinking. The coverage of the war for Nicaragua in the American media was comprehensive and telling; the scene that seemed to impress him most deeply was the shelling of Estelí, the small northern city that was virtually destroyed by the U.S.-trained National Guard. CBS showed heartbreaking footage of rebel patrols composed entirely of children, and large numbers of young people were said to have been summarily shot by government troops, on the grounds that in the present crisis citizens in their age group were "assumed to be enemies of the state." It was at an earlier point in this struggle, when it still looked as if Somoza would last forever, that Hunter made his decision to study folk music in Guatemala. I do not believe he lied about his purposes, though I do think that at the time his true reasons may have been unclear even to himself. He had begun to grow impatient with his work; he wanted to do something completely new, and so he applied for an OAS intercultural grant to do field work among the Indians of El Quiché, imagining, I think, that in those picturesque surroundings, still relatively unexplored by Folkways, he might come closer to understanding the social origins of music. I remember feeling relief at the time to hear he had chosen Guatemala, with its stable government and relatively passive indigenous population; now, of course, the irony is almost too much to bear.

It must be admitted that Hunter's career as a medievalist had been pursued by him with something less than total attention. His thesis was the best work I've seen for a young man his age—even threatening to eclipse my own work in the same area. But he never did revise it for publication in book form. As the seventies wore on, it seemed harder and harder for Hunter to take his academic duties seriously; during his tenure fight, some of his colleagues remarked to me that he seemed immature, not only because of his sparse publishing record but for more personal reasons which they really had no right to examine, like the fact that he was well over thirty and still living in Cambridge with his parents. Nobody on the committee ever got wind of Bange, luckily (it would have destroyed his chances); he had offered to marry her in 1976 when they found she was pregnant, but she told him marriage was stupid, and so he kept on as a kind of boarder in the parental home, seeming to be caught somewhere between childhood and maturity—like so many academics—and the boy Rudolph was born and flourished with a father who came and went and whose last name he would never bear. As far as the Advisory Committee was concerned, Hunter was just another aging boy with a useful flair for teaching, good connections, and no particularly damning qualities—and so his tenure finally came through. Looking back on it now, it seems improbable.

Without wanting to agree with the more intractable members of the committee, I would still have to say that Hunter's lack of socialization was a real problem. He was often difficult and moody with me (though he could be utterly charming when he liked), and when he talked about his relationship to society, he sounded curiously like an exile missing his homeland. I gather that as a child he had been of the retiring type—constantly embarrassed by his own materiality, inclined toward activities in which social relations are not critical (he loved

The Teacher

riding, so his parents had bought him a horse and paid for lessons). Clearly, this was an aspect of Hunter's childhood he had not yet managed to outgrow. His imagination in times of stress grew vivid and feverish; I remember sessions in my office during the tenure fiasco when he would describe horrible nightmares—in one that recurred he was in danger of being suffocated by balls of horsehair, clotted with blood, pursuing him down endless hills—with such conviction and drama that one was as good as drawn into his dream and suffering by his side.

These attacks were troublesome but infrequent until about the time of Rudi's birth (May of '77), when Hunter's dream life took on an obsessive cast that was really alarming. One of his passions as a child had been to study the civilizations of Mesoamerica, and these stored-up, half-forgotten images now combined with his musical training to form a stubborn pathology. Whenever he closed his eyes, whether he fell asleep immediately or not, he found himself deep in the tropics surrounded by a strange, almost inaudible music that seemed to come from everywhere at once and which was somehow in counterpoint to Bange's soft Bavarian lullabies. The soughing forests became a jungle of limbs, scores of dark-skinned indigenes, their women, their deep-eyed children, a whole race of men making music in a way Hunter couldn't understand (just by walking to market or killing a pig or making love), and whenever he asked them how it was done (in the dream he spoke Maya-Quiché), people said, *You must fight for us, Yankee,* and he obediently assumed the fatigues and field equipment of the local liberation forces and began roving the countryside with a band of Quiché and mestizo comrades (including one Jesuit priest), some of whom had been in the hills since the fall of Arbenz—a full quarter of a century.

One of the guerrillas was a young woman who reminded Hunter of Bange. In some of the dreams he was intimate with this woman; her thighs were lethal and delicious; they made love watchfully in the interstices of that illegal life, knowing that a moment's forgetfulness could mean death. In other dreams the woman really was Bange, but with an Amerindian cast to her face, her hair like falling water, the boy Rudolph riding bravely on her back like the hero of some future day. Once a band of paramilitaries attacked the camp in the predawn hours; the leader, who was recognized as a member of the local chamber of commerce, knocked William to the ground with a horsewhip, ordered Bange to follow him with the baby, and disappeared with them into the mist. In the next dream, they were back again as if nothing had happened. The locale varied; sometimes they would be deep in the warm mahogany forests of the Petén, walking along a riverbed of moss-covered rocks that glowed in the sun like carven jade, on their way to gather supplies that came overland via Belize or Campeche; at other times they might be hiding in the nervous shadow of Tajumulco, the sleeping volcano, or tramping through the mountains of the ancient kingdom of Xelaju, or hard by the Lago de Izabal with its unrepeatable greens and soft clouds of skittering white waterbirds. Once the band lived for three days on *axayácatl,* an edible mountain butterfly. (It's not entirely clear to me how much of this came from Hunter's memories of old *National Geographic*s and what may have been pure invention.) The fellow was steeped in the fierce algebra of revolution; every cotton plantation they burned was faithfully balanced by the founding of a rural cooperative in the same area. In one variation, Hunter was awakened in the camp by Billy, the horse he had ridden as a child, a gentle ungainly chestnut, white star on its brow, eyes like mossy lakewater; when he tried to mount it, the beast shied back, snuffling and whining, so that after several attempts Hunter gave up in exhaustion and tied the horse to his ankle so it wouldn't wander off as he slept. But instead of staying still, the horse dragged Hunter halfway up the mountain during the night—and when the dream-morning dawned, he was in great pain and covered with dust and blood, lying helpless on the ground, lacerated, thinking, *I must be close to death*, and the animal was looking down on him with its strange green eyes as if to say, *You always were*; and when he managed to wake up out of all that, he was still in his parents' house in Cambridge, sweating heavily and very cold, his eyes swollen with tears of self-pity, afraid he had lost the music forever.

And so the months passed and William applied for his fellowship. I was struck by the coincidence between his dream life and the area he had chosen to work in, but said nothing about it, imagining he must have his reasons. Eventually, the grant came through, and one day, incredibly, it was time for Hunter to go. He came into the office to say goodbye, looking unaccountably guilty; I wished him luck and shook his hand for what was to be the last time. He avoided mentioning Bange on this occasion, and I assumed he expected me to take her and the boy under my wing while he was gone, which I would have been glad to do. But in fact they left for Guatemala themselves a few days later. I kept trying to reach them in Cambridge and didn't discover where they'd gone, or why, until William's letters began arriving and I learned the full extent of the disaster: Bange had recruited him for the Guerrilla Army of the Poor, and now all three of them were out in the mountains fighting their dubious revolution, armed like bandits, in danger of their lives.

Bange and Rudi had flown to Managua and gone the rest of the way overland, because she felt there was a fairly good chance of being recognized by immigration at the airport at Guatemala City. For her, even so, the trip was easy, because her loyalties were firmly established. For William, it seems to have been crucially difficult. From the tone of his letter, I suspect his full conversion to the left may not have taken place until he was actually on the plane, amazed at his own decision, sitting next to "a ham-radio operator with purple suede shoes"; he was overtaken by self-doubt, he says, and had to make an enormous effort not to bolt back into the airport as the deep strangeness of his adventure, the possibility of dying violently under a foreign sky, began to impress itself upon him.

As the plane left Logan, the sun was setting, in the deep red color peculiar to industrial cities, and he was relieved to feel that his decision had become irreversible. Through the night they flew, over vast invisible fields and soundless rivers; he talked to his seatmate about personal investment opportunities; he slept, not even rousing himself for the odd-smelling meal the stewardess tried to serve him. It was still dark when the plane touched down at Dallas. The man next to him said goodbye here and left. As the plane took off again, Hunter was jolted into full wakefulness; now every detail of the huge Pan American aircraft seemed unnaturally significant, though of what he could not say: the sensible pressure in the cabin, the thin endless stream of indecisive music, the tiny sealed windows, the emergency exits with directions in

The Teacher

four languages. Down to the left he could see the Gulf, gleaming like black matte vinyl under a yellow moon, then a vague landmass that he knew must be the northern coast of Yucatán, and finally the strange pastels of dawn in Guatemala City, a wash of pink and blue beyond the landing lights.

At the gate he was met by the representative of the Party, an old friend of Bange's. Hunter suddenly felt acutely nervous, as if he hadn't talked to a human being for as long as he could remember (though in fact he had spoken at length to his fellow traveler). Would the words come?

"*Viva la revolución,*" said this friendly man, clapping Hunter three times on the back in a half-embrace. It was his first *abrazo.*

"*Vivan los compañeros,*" Hunter managed to stammer.

What were they doing, talking this way in a public airport?

The man laughed, as if he had expected this initial embarrassment. Taking William's suitcase in hand, he led him outside, to where other comrades were waiting in an old De Soto.

Hunter liked them all on the spot; they seemed to accept him as one of their own, and inundated him with marvelous lilting conversation of a kind he had never heard before, full of ironic cadences in seeming counterpoint to an open sense of purpose—"the first time I had ever experienced such a thing" (a remark that is patently unjust). All morning long they drove him through endless spirals of mountain roads; once he was able to look down and see eagles circling a thousand feet below. Around noon they reached the contact point west of Nebaj. From here, other comrades, Cubans this time, led him on foot to a secret training camp, and his life was as good as over.

This news was like a massive electric shock to me. As I read the first few lines, I thought he must have gone crazy. But Hunter anticipated my feelings, and explained his defection and Bange's part in it with such high spirits and persuasive logic that I was at least partially disarmed. It was even more surprising, then, when his second letter arrived—some six weeks later, around Christmas—and I learned that he had proceeded to ferret out the contacts we had originally set up as a support system for his grant project, and that he indeed planned to record native music as he came across it, whatever his other activities might be. I had not mentioned Hunter's true situation to anyone, of course—I could disapprove of what my student was doing with all my heart and still not wish to be an informer—so it seems that checks signed by sturdy anti-Communists at the OAS kept right on coming to Hunter's maildrop until the day of his death. The irony was not lost on him, and I must say I couldn't help laughing too, though it meant my own tax dollars were helping to finance the overthrow of a friendly government.

The life he lived from that moment on was not very different from the obsessive dream life he had experienced in Cambridge—unless the descriptions he sent me were merely literary projections of what he had already known in dreams. He was reunited with Bange and the boy before the week was out. The patrol they were assigned to worked mostly in El Quiché province, radicalizing the Indians with a fair amount of success (for the first time in history), in spite of frenetic opposition from the Lucas

The Teacher

García government and its allies. It seems the CIA is everywhere in those hills. One agent was dressed up as a native, with makeup and full indigenous costume, so that everyone around Nebaj was convinced he must be a beggar from some distant tribe; one day Hunter asked the fellow to sing the songs of his people for the tape recorder, and of course he couldn't. But Hunter insisted, and finally the man cursed Hunter out in perfect American English and ran away. Of course, as William says in the letter in question, not all his encounters with the agency were this cordial, and we think the CIA must have had a hand in his death, so in the end it's no laughing matter.

After January there were no more letters, but before long I had news of a different kind. You may remember that in February the American embassy in Guatemala City was briefly occupied by a group led by a man called Comandante Ahual, a formidable Indian giant from Chichicastenango who has since become widely known in the area. I don't recall how they got in, but it was fast and bloodless. They took the ambassador hostage at gunpoint and ordered everyone else out, then sent word that one journalist and one photographer would be permitted to enter the compound and conduct an interview in the ambassador's office; the newsmen took a vote and sent Alan Riding of the *Times*. The next morning, February 14, the world was presented with a photograph of the Comandante flanked by my two ex-students, Comrade William and Comrade Bange, he brandishing an AK-47 and a portable Sony tape recorder, she cradling a shiny new Kalashnikov (in a pose so fetching that she must have converted a million readers to the cause just by standing there). Between William and Ahual one can see the boy Rudolph sitting on the ambassador's desk, happily destroying a rather large number of what look like Havana cigars. Of the whole group, Hunter is the only one smiling; I must admit I never saw him look so happy in Cambridge. I was stunned.

Riding referred to Hunter as "Lieutenant Ducol-ri," with no attempt to guess his real identity. But with Bange it was a very different matter. Riding not only discounted the name she had been assigned by Ahual ("la Pattaskabia") and identified her correctly, but asserted that "Bange Tage" was the nom de guerre of an ex-mistress of Andreas Baader.* Ahual gave a short speech on government repression, and then Hunter read aloud several of the more embarrassing documents from the rifled files. After that, it was time for what Ahual described as a "People's Interrogation"—at which words the poor ambassador turned pale as chalk—but as soon as Riding and the photographer left, the guerrillas gagged the old man and tied him to his desk and disappeared into the executive entrance of the embassy's escape tunnel, coming out on the south side of the city free and clear as the Guatemalan Security Police were still trying to decide whether to contact Washington for instructions, or just to storm the office on their own and risk losing millions in foreign aid.

It was not long before the State Department figured out who "Lieutenant Ducol-ri" was. They immediately cancelled his passport and started proceedings to deprive him of citizenship.

It was on the very day he would have lost it, the date of the hearing in absentia at the Kennedy Building in Boston (April 16), that Hunter met his horrible death under the American guns, martyr to a doctrine I am still unable to name without feeling nausea.

* The *Times* supplies her real name, but I think it would only compound the damage to reproduce it here.

The Teacher

The group was on its way to the house of a general who was known to be the head of the local *escuadrón de la muerte*, a man who was supposedly responsible for several hundred mutilation deaths over the past eighteen months. (One of the *compañeras* had been raped and tortured by him a year earlier.) The idea was to try to politely dissuade the general from pursuing his nefarious activities, or, failing that, to "blow his head off" (Bange). They were around the altitude at which cane gives way to coffee, somewhere on a sunny road in the low hills to the west of Quezaltenango, where the pastures seemed to be strung with veils of grass and butterflies, the dreamy peaks smoking in the near distance, and everyone in good spirits, riding together on fine fresh horses. To pass the time, William began to sing some Machaut, very loud, in his rich deep baritone. Suddenly, the landscape turned ambiguous and electric as if something were wrong. No one could say what. But Hunter kept right on singing, as if defiantly.

The M-16s cut him down without any warning.

They literally blew him off his horse.

The stunned comrades tried to return the fire as they rode full-tilt toward cover, never getting more than a glimpse of their attackers, and then they scattered and were lost and it was all over.

This information comes from Bange; I practically had to force it out of her. What she hasn't told me is how she and Rudi escaped with their lives (it was fantastically lucky that the child was not riding with William at the time of the ambush), and in the days that followed, how they re-entered this country and under what name, and how it was possible for her to obtain a visa at all after her picture had been published in every major newspaper in the world.

But of course there are a lot of unanswered questions: Why was Hunter the only one hit by the bullets if so many troops opened fire at once from close range? And how did it happen, as I found out later, that the hearings on his citizenship status were cancelled less than an hour after his death? Did the man who shot him run to a phone and call Boston to tell the judge not to waste his time?

When I ask Bange these things, she just looks at me, her chameleon eyes welling with tears and resentment, and says nothing.

* * *

In these few pages I have tried to tell the story of a man who wanted to help the less fortunate of his brothers on earth, not because I believe in what he did particularly but because I loved him—that is to say, for purely sentimental reasons. Hunter's death was romantic and unnecessary—a waste—but it may yet have a certain political utility; he was fighting, after all, for social justice, an ideal we all approve of in theory but which our lives consistently deny, and perhaps it's not such a bad thing to have our consciences jogged from time to time by an extravagant personal sacrifice like Hunter's.

I freely admit that my own life—in contrast to his—is utterly indefensible: buying imported Brie at the gourmet market, standing tongue-tied in front of my sneering counterpoint class, leading perfunctory applause at Symphony on Friday afternoons.

I have never been more depressed at the spectacle of my own gentility.

Sometimes I think that I will change my life. But it is of course absurd to think so. I come from a tradition that uses wealth to deny the body, and I have always lived as though I were invisible, without weight or circum-

The Teacher

stance. Now I perceive that my inheritance as a man is a gross materiality.

Did Hunter suffer these thoughts too? Is that what drove him away?

Why do I feel so profoundly guilty?

In thinking about our present situation in Cambridge, I have begun to realize how impossible it is. Bange, as I keep reminding myself, is an international criminal, and yet she is living a normal life with no attempt at disguise or deceit. No one makes a move to arrest her; it follows that someone very powerful must be protecting her.

I have a strong feeling that this true story I set out to tell is, after all, erroneous and incomplete, because I intuit that the crucial details, the ones that would gather and explain all others, are precisely the ones I'll never know. Bange, the only one who could tell me, will not so much as fill in the real story of her origins, blithely expecting me to be content with the hastily contrived set of inventions she presented me with when we first met.

Are we all planning to be infantile forever?

Sometimes I imagine Hunter as a boy who never grew up, who kept trying to mount a balky horse, and failed—and in the end was dragged to death in the tangled stirrup of his own childhood. It must mean something that he died in a region where the worst of all crimes is to be young. I keep wondering whether there was anything in my pedagogical methods that could have led him to such an end (perhaps when I agreed to study Eisler's proletarian songs with him?). In what does my guilt consist? He changed; I am the same. He was killed; I am alive. Bange, the lovely Bange, has come back home where she belongs; she has become my wife, and I am helping her bring up the child as if he were my own.

Is that wrong?

For my part, I have never been quite so happy. I forget everything on her moving belly, her small dark body sweetly happening under mine. Is my pleasure heightened by the knowledge that she has blood on her hands?

The other night, as we undressed, I asked her what had become of the torturer, whether the ambush had saved his life. She gave me a big grin. "I got him before I left," she said. In the hours after the attack, prevented from reaching Hunter's body and hot for revenge, Bange said she had put her rifle in a gunny sack and—with Rudi riding on her back in the sling, a detail that in addition to her small size made her look completely innocuous—had gone to the general's house that very evening, walked straight in the front door without meeting anyone and out again into the central patio, where the man was strumming pedantically on a small guitar, sitting alone in a pool of yellow light. Bange said the fellow looked up in surprise and sudden terror as she aimed for his left eye and shot him dead.

The Kalashnikov went back in the grain bag. Rudi began to cry. Running outside, Bange managed to melt easily into a crowd of neighbors shouting to each other to catch the man who did this.

Like most of Bange's stories, when she tells them at all, this one ended petulantly in the middle. "Make love to me, will you?" she said. So we lay down and I held her close and kissed her as her heart pounded, molding myself to the hot body of this woman who had killed. For the first time, I seemed to comprehend my own mortality.

It was over very fast. We lay together obstinately for a while as little Rudi, alone in the next room, cried as if he had been most foully betrayed; and when he finally

The Teacher

fell asleep, she seemed happier and seduced me all over again, gently this time, drawing her thick brown hair that smells like grass back and forth across my chest.

"How can you make love to me so sweetly when I'm supposed to disgust you?" I asked her.

"You don't disgust me at all."

"If you say I deserve to be strangled in my sleep?"

"David," she said patiently, "I love *you*; I only hate what you *are*."

I don't understand this very well. The distinction seems infinitesimal. What will happen when it evaporates? But perhaps it's all just talk. Times change, and people with them.

By now I'm utterly dependent on Bange and the boy, and I hope I'll never have to lose them for any reason. In asking them to live with me, I intentionally destroyed the most precious possession I had: my ecstatic solitude. I don't miss it; I simply wait for a new reality to grow where the old one died. Some things do bother me, of course; my young helpmeet seems to have lost all her zest for accomplishment; I have tried to ask her as tactfully as possible about her plans for the future, since she hasn't wanted to go back to her old job at the social service agency and doesn't seem to have anything else in mind. There is excellent day care available. I think getting out of the house would be good for her, but I don't insist—and so instead of working, Bange spends her days at home reading and writing and playing with the child.

It is a great joy to get home from the university after a long day, to see them together, she cross-legged on the sofa lost in her Bukharin, Rudi sitting next to her like a cherub or else playing excitedly with his favorite toy, a plastic machine gun from Mattel. Sometimes, with an expression heartbreakingly reminiscent of his father, the boy lifts the weapon defiantly and pretends to shoot me through the heart. I must admit I find it mildly disturbing. I have been trying to teach him never to point the thing at anybody, even in fun.

About the Author

William Ferguson attended Phillips Academy, Andover, and took his doctorate at Harvard in Spanish literature, which subject he now teaches at Clark University. He has founded two fine presses, more recently Metacom, and has, in this connection, brought out limited editions of work by such writers as Ann Beattie, John McPhee, and John Updike, and such poets as James Tate and Diane Wakoski.

A Note on the Type

The text of this book was set on the Linotype in a face called Primer, designed by Rudolph Ruzicka, who was earlier responsible for the design of Fairfield and Fairfield Medium, Linotype faces whose virtues have for some time now been accorded wide recognition. The complete range of sizes of Primer was first made available in 1954, although the pilot size of 12-point was ready as early as 1951. The design of the face makes general reference to Linotype Century—long a serviceable type, totally lacking in manner or frills of any kind —but brilliantly corrects its characterless quality.

This book was composed by Maryland Linotype Composition Co., Inc., Baltimore, Maryland. It was printed and bound by The Haddon Craftsmen, Inc., Scranton, Pennsylvania.

Design by Judith Henry